HOPSCOTCH HISTORIES

# Eric Bloodaxe, the Viking King

by Damian Harvey

Illustrated

## About this book

The story and some of the characters are made up
but the subject is based upon real events in history.
Eric Bloodaxe appears in many Viking stories but little is
known about his real life. He is thought to have been the
last independent king of Northumbria, gaining the throne
in 947 or 948. His name conjures up typical Viking
imagery and he was known to wield a mighty axe. His
wife, Gunnhild, was often depicted as a witch. He died in
about 954 in a battle at Stainmore, which brought an end
to independent Viking rule in Northumbria.

First published in 2009 by
Franklin Watts
338 Euston Road
London
NW1 3BH

Franklin Watts Australia
Level 17/207 Kent Street
Sydney
NSW 2000

Text © Damian Harvey 2009
Illustrations © Ross Collins 2009

The right of Damian Harvey to be identified as the author
and Ross Collins as illustrator of this Work has been asserted
in accordance with the Copyright, Designs and Patents Act, 1988.

Eric Bloodaxe was a fierce
Viking king. Not many people
know his real story – except me.

My father was a blacksmith.
He was busy making a special
helmet for Eric.

My brother Ulrik was mending
the roof, while I looked after
the sheep and lambs.

Suddenly, the door burst open. It was Gunnhild, Eric's wife. She was the scariest woman I'd ever seen!

"Where's Eric's helmet?" she screeched. "Is it ready yet?"

"Nearly," replied my father.

"Work faster!" Gunnhild shouted, "Eric needs it tomorrow when he meets Lord Oswulf."

"He needs to look his best –
and scariest!" she said,
storming off.

My father worked all night to make sure the helmet was ready. I saw it as soon as I woke up.

"You must take this to King Eric,"
he told me. "I have to start
sharpening these axes."

I grabbed the helmet and rushed to the Great Hall, where King Eric and Queen Gunnhild lived.

Lots of people were gathering
there, waiting to see their king.

I bumped into my brother Ulrik. "Eric will be named king of all Northumbria by Lord Oswulf. We're going to join them," he said.

I wanted to go too but
Ulrik wouldn't let me.
"You're too young," he said.

As the Viking warriors rode away,
I saw Gunnhild staring at me. Then
I realised that I still had the helmet!

I ran after the warriors as fast
as I could, but it was too late.
They were already far away.

I ran through forests and across moors. I had to find King Eric before he met Lord Oswulf.

When I found them, the warriorrs were getting ready for battle. The horses were stamping their feet. Battle cries filled the air.

"We've been tricked!" cried Ulrik.

"Lord Oswulf wants to kill Eric so he can become king instead. He's sent a huge army to fight us."

I wanted to fight as well, but someone stopped me. I looked up and saw the long red beard of Eric Bloodaxe.

"Here is your helmet," I said.
"What a fine helmet it is," Eric
boomed. "You can borrow it while
you look after your lamb."

Then Eric put the helmet on
my head, picked up his axe
and rode away.

I watched as Eric went into battle.
My brother was at his side.

Everyone said that Eric Bloodaxe fought bravely, but I never saw him alive again.

That night the warriors returned
with Eric's body. We laid him on
a stone with all his weapons,
including the helmet he never wore.

# Puzzle 1

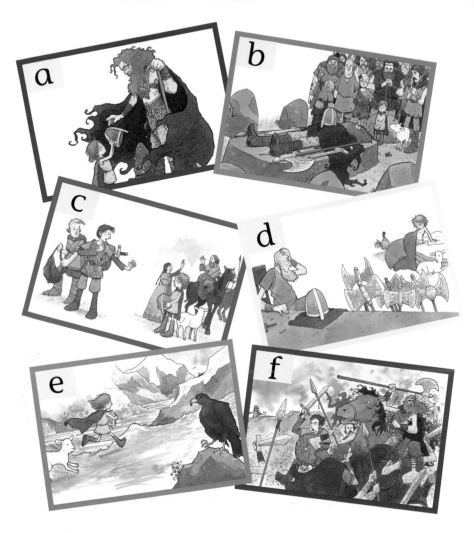

Put these pictures in the correct order.

Which event do you think is most important?

Now try writing the story in your own words!

# Puzzle 2

## Word Bank

Army
Axes
Battle
Helmet
Sheep
Warrior

What do these pictures tell you about

Vikings and the way of life at the time?

How are things different today?

You can use the word bank to help you.

# Answers

## Puzzle 1

The correct order is: 1d, 2c, 3e, 4a, 5f, 6b.

## Puzzle 2

Life was very different in Viking times.

Think about homes, jobs, armies and clothing.

To find out more, try this book:

Vikings, (Children in History), Kate Jackson Bedford, Franklin Watts, 2009

**Look out for more Hopscotch Histories:**

**Henry VIII Has to Choose**
ISBN 978 0 7496 8573 7*
ISBN 978 0 7496 8579 9

**The King and the Great Fire**
ISBN 978 0 7496 8575 1*
ISBN 978 0 7496 8581 2

**Florence and the Drummer Boy**
ISBN 978 0 7496 8574 4*
ISBN 978 0 7496 8580 5

**Ben's Escape from the Blitz**
ISBN 978 0 7496 8578 2*
ISBN 978 0 7496 8584 3

**The Song of Boudica**
ISBN 978 0 7496 8576 8*
ISBN 978 0 7496 8582 9

**Eric Bloodaxe, the Viking King**
ISBN 978 0 7496 8577 5*
ISBN 978 0 7496 8583 6

**Toby and the Great Fire of London**
ISBN 978 0 7496 7410 6

**Hoorah for Mary Seacole**
ISBN 978 0 7496 7413 7

**Remember Remember the 5th of November**
ISBN 978 0 7496 7414 4

**Pocahontas the Peacemaker**
ISBN 978 0 7496 7080 1*
ISBN 978 0 7496 7411 3

**Grandma's Seaside Bloomers**
ISBN 978 0 7496 7412 0

**Tutankhamun and the Golden Chariot**
ISBN 978 0 7496 7084 9*
ISBN 978 0 7496 7415 1

**For more Hopscotch books go to: www.franklinwatts.co.uk**

*hardback